Favorite Mother Goose and Animal Tales

Including *The Three Little Pigs, The Three Billy Goats Gruff, The Town Mouse and the Country Mouse*

Illustrated by Ann Schweninger and Christopher Santoro

Cover art by Leonard Lubin

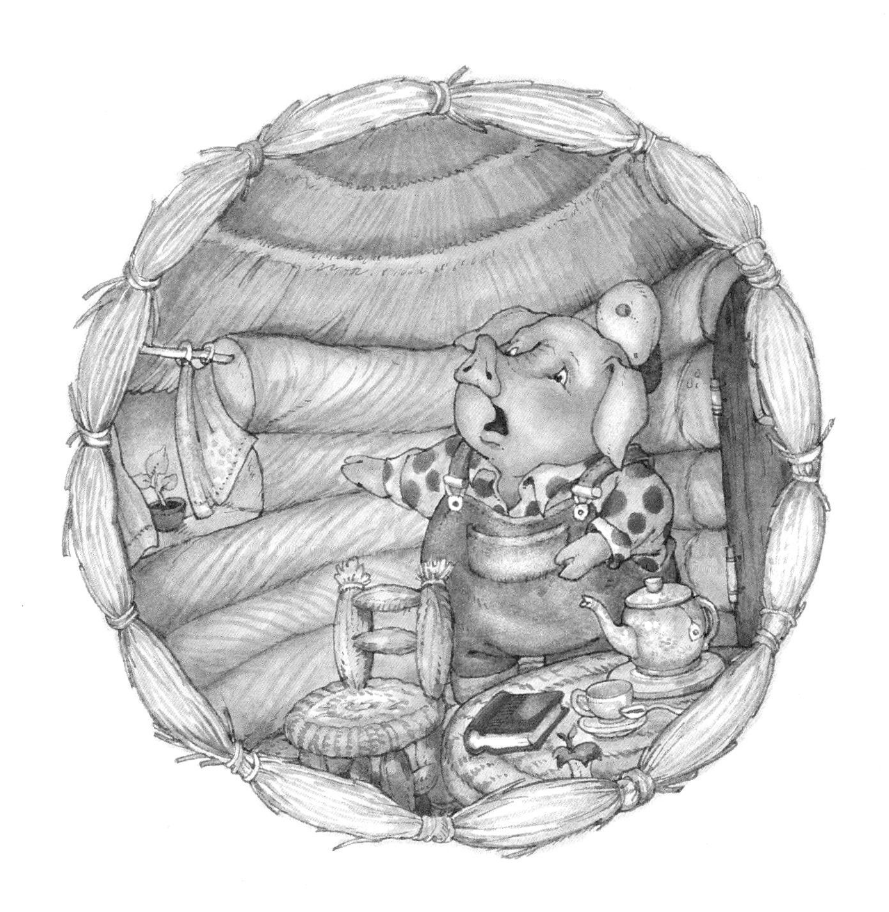

A GOLDEN BOOK • NEW YORK
Western Publishing Company, Inc., Racine, Wisconsin 53404

 Library of Congress Catalog Card Number: 89-50726
ISBN: 0-307-15822-5/ISBN: 0-307-67822-9 (lib. bdg.) A B C D E F G H I J K L M

Hey diddle, diddle,
The cat and the fiddle,
The cow jumped over the moon;
The little dog laughed
To see such sport,
And the dish ran away with the spoon.

Humpty Dumpty sat on a wall,
Humpty Dumpty had a great fall;
All the King's horses and all the King's men
Couldn't put Humpty together again.

Mary, Mary, quite contrary,
How does your garden grow?
With silver bells and cockle shells,
And pretty maids all in a row.

Ring-a-ring of roses,
A pocket full of posies,
A-tishoo! A-tishoo!
We all fall down.

The cows are in the meadow
Lying fast asleep,
A-tishoo! A-tishoo!
We all get up again.

Pat-a-cake, pat-a-cake, baker's man,
Bake me a cake as fast as you can;
Pat it and prick it, and mark it with a B,
And put it in the oven for Baby and me.

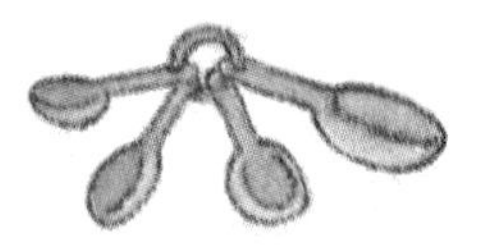

Hickory, dickory, dock,
The mouse ran up the clock.
The clock struck one,
The mouse ran down,
Hickory, dickory, dock.

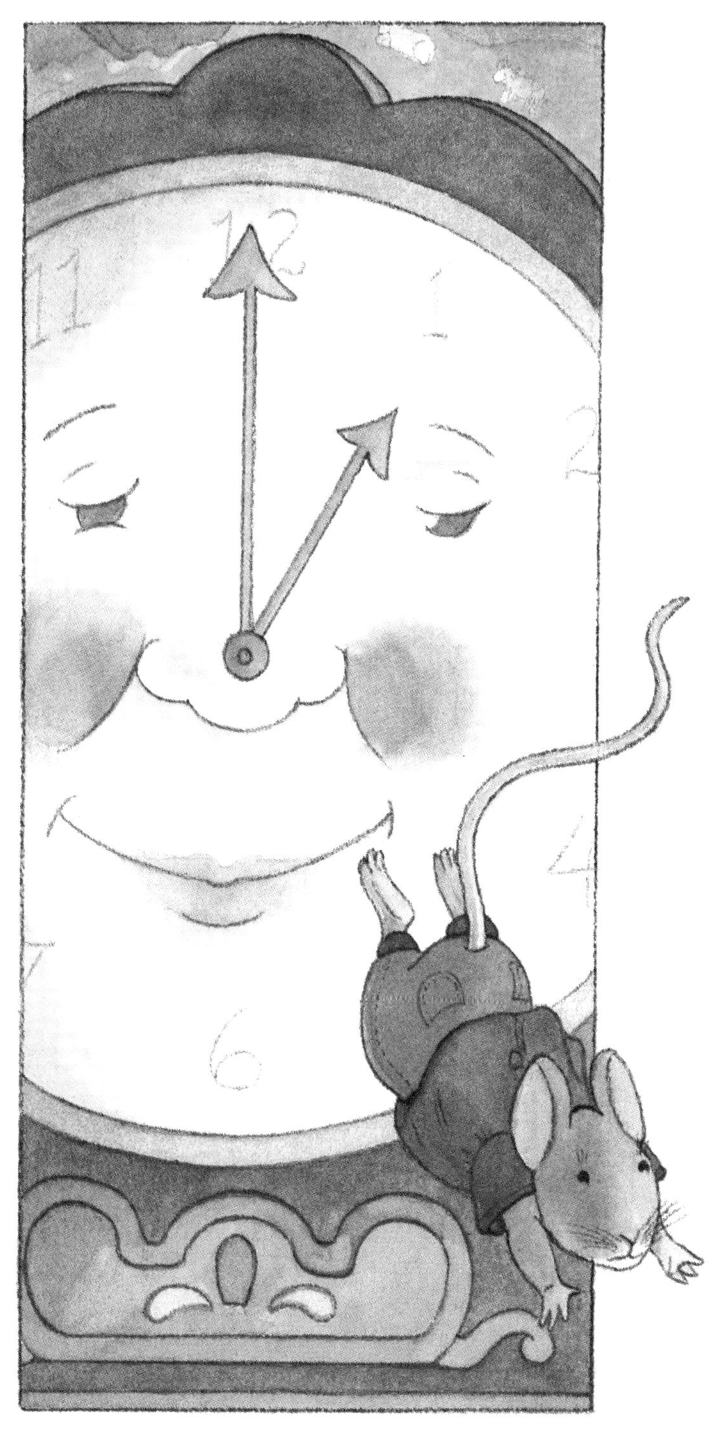

This little pig went to market,
This little pig stayed at home,
This little pig had roast beef,
This little pig had none,
And this little pig cried, Wee-wee-
wee-wee-wee,
I can't find my way home.

To market, to market,
To buy a fat pig,
Home again, home again,
Jiggety-jig.
To market, to market,
To buy a fat hog,
Home again, home again,
Jiggety-jog.

The Three Little Pigs

THERE WAS an old sow with three little pigs, and as she had not enough to keep them, she sent them out to seek their fortune.

The first that went off met a man with a bundle of straw, and said to him, "Please, man, give me that straw to build me a house."

The man did, and the little pig built a house with it.

Presently along came a wolf, who knocked at the door, and said, "Little pig, little pig, let me come in."

To which the pig answered, "Not by the hair of my chinny-chin-chin."

The wolf then answered, "Then I'll huff, and I'll puff, and I'll blow your house in."

So he huffed, and he puffed, and he blew the house in, and ate up the little pig.

The second little pig met a man with a bundle of sticks, and said, "Please, man, give me some of those sticks to build me a house."

The man did, and the little pig built his house.

Then along came the wolf, and said, "Little pig, little pig, let me come in."

"Not by the hair of my chinny-chin-chin."

"Then I'll puff, and I'll huff, and I'll blow your house in."

So he huffed, and he puffed, and he puffed, and he huffed, and at last he blew the house down, and he ate up the little pig.

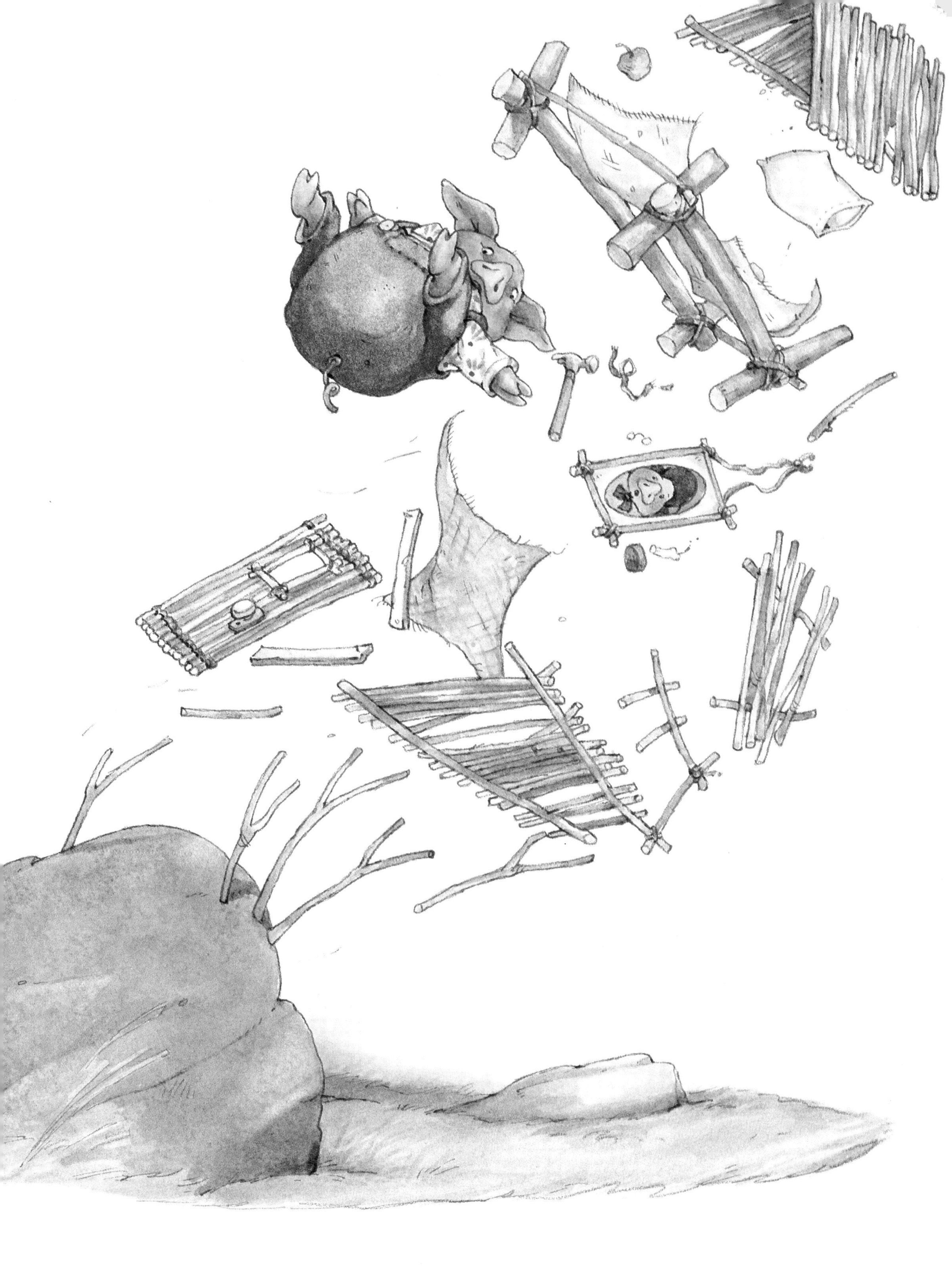

The third little pig met a man with a load of bricks, and said, "Please, man, give me those bricks to build me a house."

So the man gave him the bricks, and he built his house with them.

So the wolf came, as he did to the other little pigs, and said, "Little pig, little pig, let me come in."

"Not by the hair of my chinny-chin-chin."

"Then I'll huff, and I'll puff, and I'll blow your house in."

Well, he huffed, and he puffed, and he huffed, and he puffed, but he could *not* get the house down.

When he found that he could not, with all his huffing and puffing, blow the house down, he said, "Little pig, I know where there is a nice field of turnips."

"Where?" said the little pig.

"Oh, in Mr. Smith's field. And if you will be ready tomorrow morning, I will call for you, and we will go together and get some for dinner."

"Very well," said the little pig. "I will be ready. What time do you mean to go?"

"Oh, at six o'clock."

Well, the little pig got up at five and got the turnips before the wolf came and said, "Little pig, are you ready?"

The little pig said, "Ready! I have been and come back again and got a nice potful for dinner."

The wolf felt very angry at this, but thought that he could outsmart the little pig somehow or other, so he said, "Little pig, I know where there is a nice apple tree."

"Where?" said the pig.

"Down at Merry-Garden," replied the wolf. "And if you will not deceive me, I will come for you at five o'clock tomorrow and get some apples."

Well, the little pig bustled up the next morning at four o'clock, and went off for the apples, hoping to get back before the wolf came. But he had far to go and had to climb the tree, so that just as he was coming down from it, he saw the wolf coming, which, as you may suppose, frightened him very much.

When the wolf came up he said, "What, little pig! Are you here before me? Are they nice apples?"

"Yes, very," said the little pig. "I will throw you down one."

And he threw it so far that, while the wolf went to pick it up, the little pig jumped down and ran home.

The next day the wolf came again, and said to the little pig, "Little pig, there is a fair at Shanklin this afternoon. Will you go?"

"Oh, yes," said the pig. "I will go. What time shall you be ready?"

"At three," said the wolf.

So the little pig went off before the time, as usual, and got to the fair and bought a butter churn. He was going home with the churn when he saw the wolf coming. Then he could not tell what to do. So he got into the churn to hide, and by so doing turned it round, and it rolled down the hill with the pig in it, which frightened the wolf so much that he ran home without going to the fair.

He went to the little pig's house and told him how frightened he had been by a great round thing that came down the hill past him.

Then the little pig said, "I frightened you then. I had been to the fair and bought a butter churn. And when I saw you, I got into it, and rolled down the hill."

The wolf was very angry indeed, and declared he would eat up the little pig, and that he would get down the chimney after him.

When the little pig saw what he was doing, he filled his biggest pot full of water and hung it over the fire. Then, just as the wolf was coming down, he took off the cover. The wolf fell into the boiling water, and that was the end of him. And the little pig lived happily ever afterwards.

Tom, Tom, the piper's son,
Stole a pig and away he run;
The pig was eat,
And Tom was beat,
And Tom went howling down the street.

Yankee Doodle went to town
A-riding on a pony;
He stuck a feather in his cap
And called it macaroni.

Yankee Doodle keep it up,
Yankee Doodle dandy,
Mind the music and the step,
And with the girls be handy.

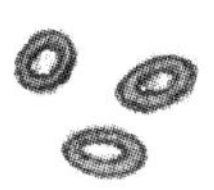

Ride a cock-horse to Banbury Cross,
To see a fine lady upon a white horse;
Rings on her fingers and bells on her toes,
And she shall have music wherever she goes.

Little Miss Muffet
Sat on a tuffet,
Eating her curds and whey;
Along came a spider,
And sat down beside her
And frightened Miss Muffet away.

Little Jack Horner
Sat in a corner,
Eating a Christmas pie;
He put in his thumb,
And pulled out a plum,
And said, What a good boy am I!

There was a crooked man,
And he walked a crooked mile,
He found a crooked sixpence
Against a crooked stile;
He bought a crooked cat,
Which caught a crooked mouse,
And they all lived together
In a little crooked house.

The Three Billy Goats Gruff

ONCE UPON A TIME there were three Billy Goats Gruff who lived on a hillside next to a wide, deep stream.

On the other side of the stream was a field of sweet, green grass.

Every day the three Billy Goats Gruff looked hungrily at the field on the other side of the stream. Every day they longed to eat some of the sweet, green grass.

But to get to the other side of the stream, they had to cross a wooden bridge. And under the bridge lived a horrible, mean troll.

One day the littlest Billy Goat Gruff said, "I cannot wait any longer. I am going to cross the bridge and eat the sweet, green grass."

"We will come, too," said his brothers. "We will be right behind you."

Little Billy Goat Gruff started across the bridge. *Trip-trap, trip-trap* went his little hoofs on the planks of wood.

"Who is that *trip-trapping* over my bridge?" said the troll.

"It is I, Little Billy Goat Gruff," said Little Billy Goat Gruff in his wee, small voice.

"I am coming up to eat you!" roared the troll.

Little Billy Goat Gruff was afraid. "Oh, please don't eat me," he said. "Wait for my big brother. He is much larger and tastier than I am."

"Very well," said the troll, licking his lips. "You may go ahead."

So Little Billy Goat Gruff crossed the bridge and got to the field on the other side.

Then Middle Billy Goat Gruff started across the bridge. *Trip-trap, trip-trap* went his middle-sized hoofs on the planks of wood.

"Who is that *trip-trapping* over my bridge?" called the troll.

"It is I, Middle Billy Goat Gruff," said Middle Billy Goat Gruff in his middle-sized voice.

"I am coming up to eat you!" roared the troll.

Middle Billy Goat Gruff was afraid. "Please don't eat me," he said. "Wait for my big brother. He is much larger and tastier than I."

"Very well," said the troll, thinking of the fine meal he would have. "You may go ahead."

So Middle Billy Goat Gruff crossed the bridge safely and got to the field on the other side.

Then Big Billy Goat Gruff started across the bridge. *TRIP-TRAP, TRIP-TRAP* went his big hoofs on the planks of wood. The whole bridge shook with his weight.

"Who is that *TRIP-TRAPPING* over my bridge?" roared the troll in his loudest voice.

"It is I, Big Billy Goat Gruff," shouted Big Billy Goat Gruff in *his* loudest voice.

"I suppose you are going to tell me to wait for your big brother," said the troll.

"Oh, no," said Big Billy Goat Gruff. "I am the biggest one there is."

"Then I am coming up to eat you!" the troll shouted. And he climbed onto the bridge.

Big Billy Goat Gruff was not afraid. "I would like to see you try!" he said.

He rushed at the troll and butted him with his horns. The troll fell off the bridge and disappeared, leaving no trace.

After that the three Billy Goats Gruff crossed the bridge whenever they liked and ate their fill of sweet, green grass.

And the horrible, mean troll never bothered them again.

Here sits the Lord Mayor,
Here sit his men,
Here sits the cockadoodle,
Here sits the hen.
Here sit the little chickens,
Here they run in,
Chin chucker, chin chucker,
chin chucker, chin.

Pease porridge hot,
Pease porridge cold,
Pease porridge in the pot
Nine days old.
Some like it hot,
Some like it cold,
Some like it in the pot
Nine days old.

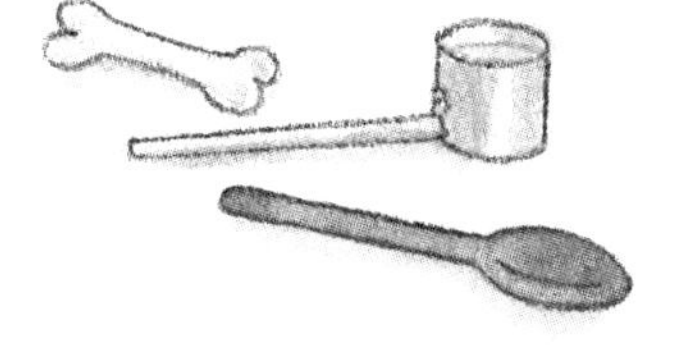

Robert Barnes, fellow fine,
Can you shoe this horse of mine?
Yes, good sir, that I can,
As well as any other man.
There's a nail and there's a prod,
And now, good sir, your horse is shod.

Jack Sprat could eat no fat,
His wife could eat no lean,
And so between them both, you see,
They licked the platter clean.

A was an apple pie

B bit it

C cut it

D dealt it

E eat it

F fought for it

G got it

H had it

I inspected it

J jumped for it

K kept it

L longed for it

M mourned for it

N nodded at it

O opened it

P peeped in it

Q quartered it

R ran for it

S stole it

T took it

U upset it

V viewed it

W wanted it

X, Y, and Z all had a large
slice and went off to bed.

1, 2,
Buckle my shoe;

3, 4,
Close the door;

5, 6,
Pick up sticks;

7, 8,
Lay them straight;

9, 10,
A big fat hen;

11, 12,
Dig and delve;

13, 14,
Maids a-courting;

15, 16,
Maids in kitchen;

17, 18,
Maids in waiting;

19, 20,
My plate's empty.

Solomon Grundy,
Born on a Monday,
Christened on Tuesday,
Married on Wednesday,
Took ill on Thursday,
Worse on Friday,
Died on Saturday,
Buried on Sunday,
This is the end
of Solomon Grundy.

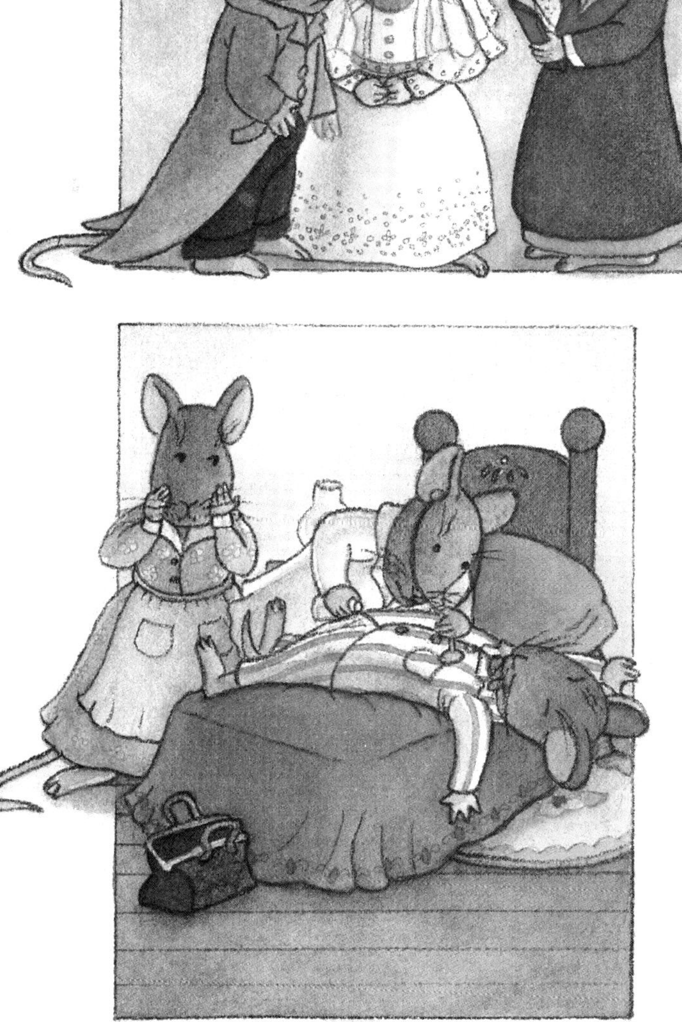

Baa, baa, black sheep,
Have you any wool?
Yes, sir, yes, sir,
Three bags full;
One for the master,
And one for the dame,
And one for the little boy
Who lives down the lane.

Little Boy Blue,
    Come blow your horn,
The sheep's in the meadow,
    The cow's in the corn.

Where is the boy
    Who looks after the sheep?
He's under a haycock
    Fast asleep.

The Town Mouse and the Country Mouse

A COUNTRY MOUSE was glad to hear that his cousin, the town mouse, was coming to dinner. He gave his cousin all the best food he had—dried beans, peas, and crusts of bread. The town mouse tried not to show how he disliked the food, and picked a little here and tasted a little there to be polite.

After dinner, he said, "How can you stand such food all the time? I suppose here in the country you don't know about anything better. Why don't you come home with me? When you have once tasted the delicious things I eat, you will never want to come back here."

The country mouse not only forgave the town mouse for disliking his dinner, but even consented to go that very evening to the city. They arrived late at night, and the town mouse took his country cousin at once to a room where there had been a big dinner.

"You are tired," he said. "Rest here, and I'll bring you some real food." And he brought the country mouse such things as nuts, dates, cake, and fruit.

The country mouse thought it was all so good that he wanted to stay there. But before he had a chance to say so, he heard a terrible roar, and looking up, he saw a huge creature dash into the room. Frightened out of his wits, the country mouse ran from the table, round and round the room, looking for a hiding place.

At last he found a safe place. While he stood there trembling, he made up his mind to go home as soon as he could get safely away. For he said to himself, "I would rather have plain food in safety than dates and nuts in the midst of danger."

Home Sweet Home

Sleep, baby, sleep,
Thy father guards the sheep;
Thy mother shakes the dreamland tree
And from it fall sweet dreams for thee,
Sleep, baby, sleep.

Sleep, baby, sleep,
Our cottage vale is deep;
The little lamb is on the green,
With woolly fleece so soft and clean—
Sleep, baby, sleep.

Wee Willie Winkie runs through the town,
Upstairs and downstairs in his nightgown,
Rapping at the window, crying through the lock,
Are the children all in bed, for now it's eight o'clock?

Diddle, diddle, dumpling, my son John,
Went to bed with his trousers on;
One shoe off, and one shoe on,
Diddle, diddle, dumpling, my son John.

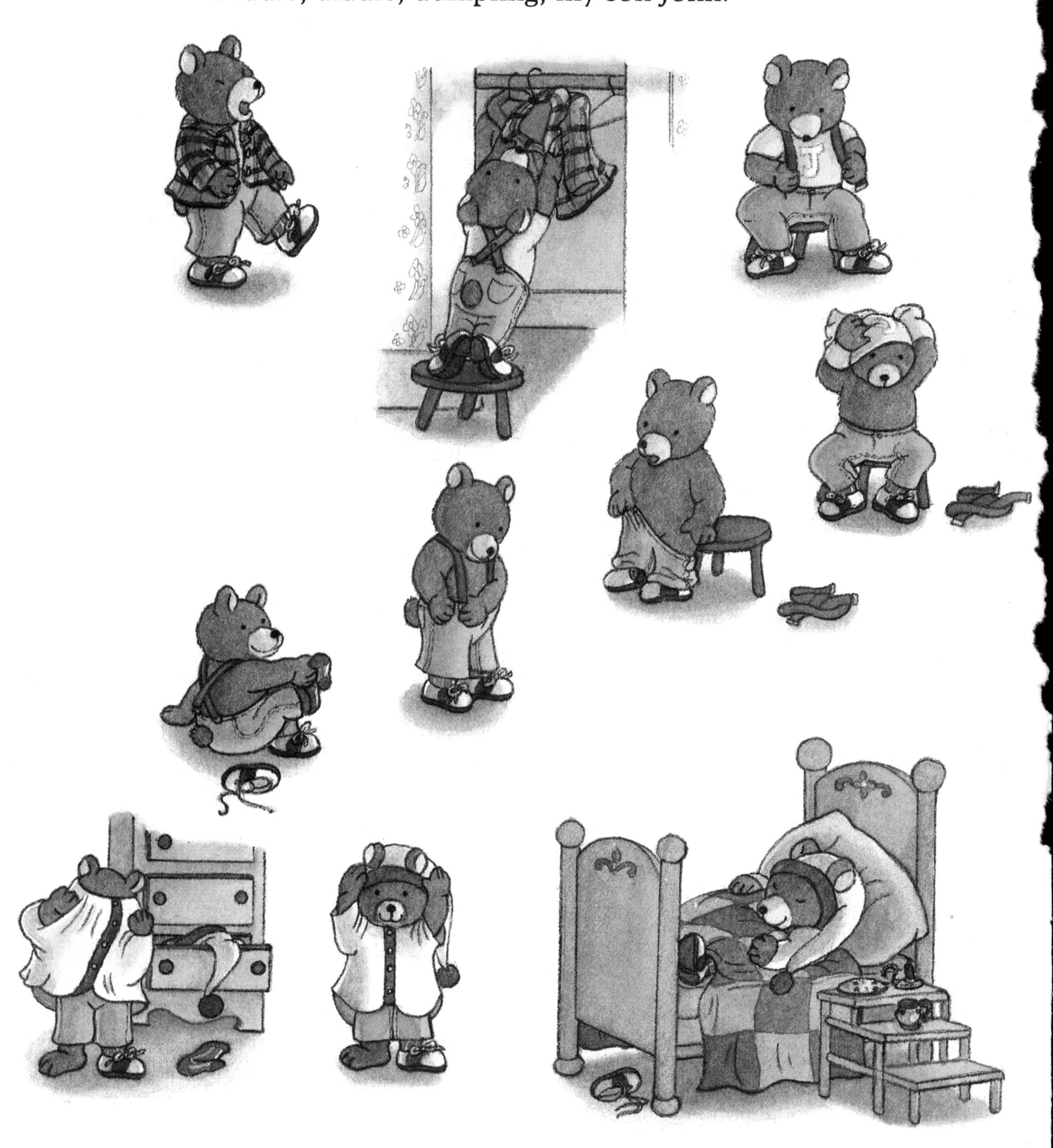